Truly
& Cheesy
Shakespeare Facts & Jokes

Published in Great Britain in MMXVIII by
Book House, an imprint of
The Salariya Book Company Ltd
25 Marlborough Place, Brighton BN1 1UB
www.salariya.com

ISBN: 978-1-912233-79-3

SALARIYA

1 3 5 7 9 8 6 4 2

A CIP catalogue record for this book is available from the British Library.

Printed and bound in Turkey.
Printed on paper from sustainable sources.

Created and designed by
David Salariya.

PAPER FROM SUSTAINABLE FORESTS

Author:
John Townsend worked as a secondary school teacher before becoming a full-time writer.
He specialises in illuminating and humorous information books for all ages.

Artist:
David Antram studied at Eastbourne College of Art and then worked in advertising for 15 years before becoming a full-time artist.
He has illustrated many children's non-fiction books.

Truly Foul & Cheesy™ Shakespeare Facts & Jokes

This Truly Foul & Cheesy
book belongs to:

....

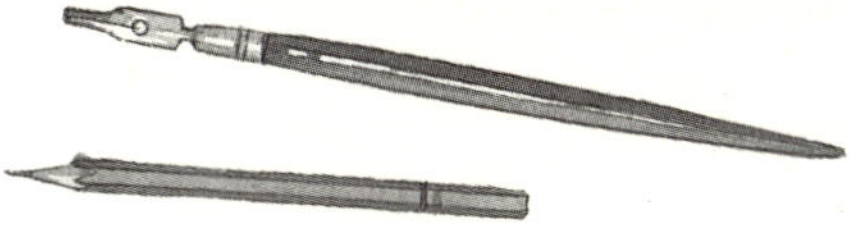

Written by
John Townsend

Illustrated by
David Antram

BOOK HOUSE
a SALARIYA imprint

Introduction

Warning – reading this book might not make you LOL (laugh out loud) but it could make you GOL (groan out loud), feel sick out loud or SEL (scream even louder). If you are reading this in a library by a SILENCE sign... get ready to be thrown out!

Disclaimer: The author really hasn't made anything up in this book (apart from some daft limericks and jokes). He checked out the foul facts as best he could and even double-checked the fouler bits to make sure – so please don't get too upset if you find out something different or meet a Shakespearean actor, someone called Bottom with an ass's head, the Queen of the Fairies or a crazy old man with a beard on the heath (or even on the chin).

Official Warning

This book contains all sorts of weird, wacky and wow snippets about William Shakespeare.
It has lots of random bits and pieces that some might find revolting and others might find fascinating – or just plain silly.

Not all the facts are foul, as Shakespeare is often called the greatest writer ever – so 'respect!' Not all his plays and poems get a mention here – there are just too many to include in a little book. So, just like the great man himself, this is a mixture of the good and the bard (yes, Shakespeare was known as the Bard of Avon).

So, pull on your tights, dab on the face-paint, leap onto the stage and enjoy the performance...

Cheesy Limerick

This book is packed full of
the Bard,
With facts – so be on
your guard...
You might laugh and howl
When the facts become foul,
And the jokes leave you
mentally scarred!

Cheesy Riddles

Q: Why was William Shakespeare always able to write great literature, however difficult?
A: Because where there's a Will, there's a way.

Reminder:

Shakespeare wrote the play *Hamlet* (first performed in 1609) about the Prince of Denmark. The most famous line is spoken when Hamlet is deciding whether to live or die: 'To be, or not to be, that is the question…' So now the daft jokes...

Q: What did Shakespeare say when cooking cheese on toast?
A: To brie or not to brie, that is the question.

Q: What did Shakespeare say when he thought about going on a diet?
A: Tubby or not tubby, that is the question.

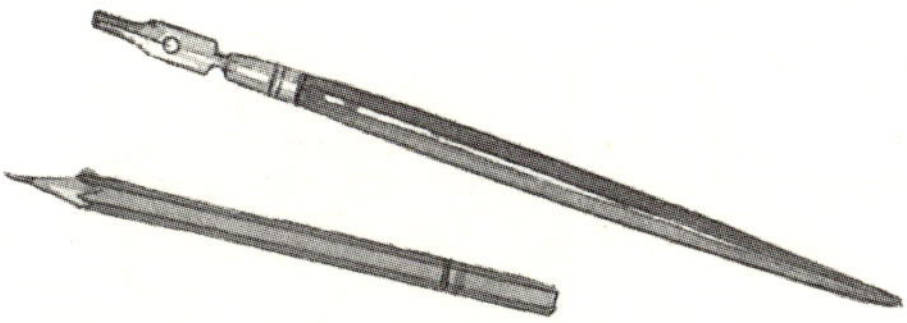

Q: What did Shakespeare say when he was deciding which pencil to use?

A: 2B or not 2B, that is the question.

Q: What did Shakespeare say when he was choosing a new pet cat?

A: Tabby or not tabby, that is the question.

Cheesy Jokes

Knock, knock.
Who's there?
Toby.
Toby who?
Toby or not Toby,
that is the question.

Knock, knock.
Who's there?
Ferris.
Ferris who?
Ferris foul and foul is fair.

Yes, 'Fair is foul and foul is fair' is said by a witch in Shakespeare's *Macbeth*. In other words, things aren't always what they seem.

In fact, Shakespeare quite liked lines that were 'foul and cheesy'. He coined the term 'foul play' in the play *Love's Labour's Lost*. In other plays, saying someone was like a cheese was an insult. So brace yourself for more truly foul and cheesy Shakespeare jokes and facts…

In the famous portrait of William Shakespeare, his head is bald on top – so he's probably asking, 'Toupee or not toupee, that is the question.'

Don't worry… the jokes might get slightly better (but not much).

FUN FACTS AND FOUL FAKERIES ABOUT WILLIAM SHAKESPEARE – which of these is totally false?

1 Shakespeare was probably born on April 23rd, 1564. However, as he was born under the old Julian calendar, what was April 23rd during Shakespeare's life would be May 3rd according to today's Gregorian calendar.

2 He was born in the town of Stratford-upon-Avon in a foul-smelling goat shed.

3 He had seven brothers and sisters and shared a bedroom with a goat.

4 He had a pet nanny goat called Ophelia, which may be why he grew a goatee beard himself. Together with his cat, he set off to London to find his fortune.

5 Shakespeare married his wife Anne Hathaway when he was 18. They had three children – a son, Hamnet, who died in 1596, and two daughters, Susanna and Judith. They had no grandchildren or goats.

6 The longest word in a Shakespeare play is honorificabilitudinitatibus in the play *Love's Labour's Lost*.

7 During his life, Shakespeare wrote at least 37 plays, 154 sonnets and other poems – even limericks. There were also some 'lost plays' and others he collaborated on. This means Shakespeare wrote an average 1.5 plays a year from when he first started writing in 1589.

8 Shakespeare made up almost 3,000 words and about half of these are now used regularly in the English language (some of them a bit rude).

9 Shakespeare's shortest play, *The Comedy of Errors*, is only a third of the length of his longest, *Hamlet*, which takes over four hours to perform.

10 Shakespeare died on 23rd April 1616 – his 52nd birthday. He was buried in Stratford-upon-Avon, although he spent much of his working life in London.

ANSWER: They're all **TRUE**, apart from no. 4 and any mention of goats! In fact, Shakespeare probably didn't like goats much as he used them as a term of insult in his play *Henry V*.

Loopy Limericks

Known by his friends as
'Bard Billy',
Young Shakespeare could
often be silly
By upsetting folks
With the cheesiest jokes
But he still churned
them out, willy-nilly.

William Shakespeare,
Known as the Bard,
Had to work day and
night very hard.
All day he would write
In the hours of daylight,
And at night, on the
stage, where he starred.

Actually, most theatre performances were in the afternoon as candles were very expensive in Shakespeare's time. Most writers wrote in the daytime and met friends after dark. Sometimes Shakespeare was busy writing one play while acting in another of his plays.

Did you know?

One of Shakespeare's relatives, William Arden, was arrested for plotting against Queen Elizabeth I. He was then imprisoned in the Tower of London and executed...ouch!

Calling Shakespeare an Elizabethan playwright isn't strictly true. Most of his plays were written after Queen Elizabeth's death, when James I was in charge (making Shakespeare more of a Jacobean writer).

Shakespeare seemed to be fond of one grisly kind of death – suicide. His characters were killing themselves all over the place – in fact, a whopping 13 times in the list of Shakespearean plays.

Time for a giggle?

Shakespeare walks into a London theatre but the manager says, 'You can't come in here, you're bard!'

Did you hear about the Shakespearean actor who stamped his foot in rage and fell through the theatre floor?
It was just a stage he was going through.

Plays in Shakespeare's time

A new theatre was built in London in 1599, called The Globe. The Globe was round and open to the sky, with a roof over the stage to keep rain off the actors but not the audience. A flag was raised to show a play was about to begin – usually at 2 o'clock in the afternoon.

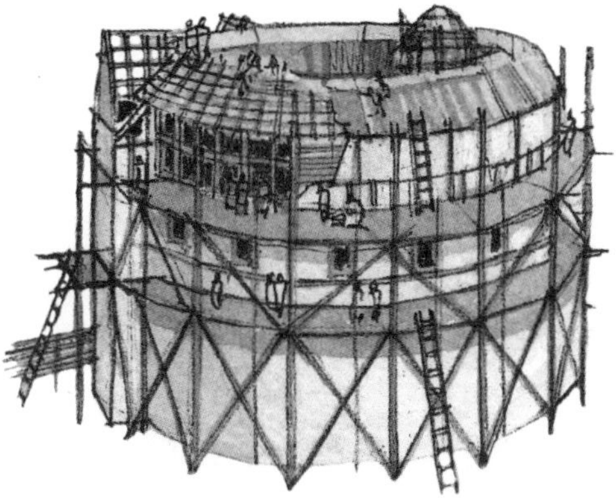

For the next 15 years, Shakespeare's plays were performed at The Globe to large crowds, including royalty. Some plays were comedies, with lots of audience shouting and cheering, while other plays were about history or faraway places that few people knew about because not many could read. The Globe opened up a new world to many Londoners.

Stink Alert

Many theatres were smelly places, particularly in front of the stage at The Globe where poorer people would stand in the rain, dirt and straw known as the pit. These people were called 'groundlings' or 'penny stinkards' as their place was cheap but smelly. Rich people paid 12 pennies (one shilling) to sit on the stage or in special decorated boxes sheltered from the weather.

Audiences were often rowdy as they shouted and clapped, laughed and booed. Sometimes they threw fruit, vegetables or anything at hand. Actors could be lowered from the roof on wires or pop up through a trap door in the stage. Other things could 'pop up', too…

Cross Alert

A few years before The Globe opened, all London playhouses were closed between 1592 and 1594 as it was thought that crowded places could spread the plague. As theatres would have been infested with rats and fleas, itchy performances probably did spread disease (not that people knew then that plague was spread by fleas). Sneezy, sweaty, flea-ridden bodies packed together would be the breeding ground for parasites and germs.

During this time when all theatres closed because of the spreading plague, there was no demand for Shakespeare's plays, so he wrote sonnets instead. These were rhyming poems of fourteen lines, such as one that starts with 'Shall I compare thee to a summer's day?' That hopefully meant warm and bright, not cold, wet and full of wind.

Bringing The House Down

Many of Shakespeare's plays used exciting special effects. There were ghosts, witches, loud bangs, flames and smoke, drums and even cannons.

In 1613, during Shakespeare's play *Henry VIII*, a cannon set fire to the straw in the roof. The Globe Theatre burned down. Oops. They said the performance was so spectacular it brought the house down!

Never mind… nearly 400 years later, a NEW Globe Theatre opened in London – near to the original site and designed just like it. The new Globe opened in 1997. The first play was *Henry V* – just as when the first Globe opened in 1599. So now you can watch plays just like Shakespeare did and you can even be a stinkard (though hopefully without the stink).

ACTORS IN SHAKESPEARE'S DAY

In Shakespeare's time, there were no female actors. Women's parts were played by boys. For a time, child actors were more popular than grown-up actors. Shakespeare acted various parts as well, including the Ghost in his play *Hamlet*. That meant white make-up – a foul mixture. Face paint was made of white lead and vinegar. That wasn't just yucky, it was deadly poisonous.

The expensive dye used to give cheeks a rosy flush and tint the lips red was cochineal. That's still used as a food dye and guess what – it's made from crushed-up bugs.

Gross Alert

Shakespeare's actors might well have used real animal blood for special effects. His early tragedy *Titus Andronicus* is yuckily gory, with one character having her tongue cut out and her hands cut off. That's a lot of gunge from the butcher flying around the stage – the stink in the summer must have been **FOUL.**

Quick Reminder

SHAKESPEARE'S PLAYS COME IN THREE MAIN GROUPS:

COMEDIES with a happy(ish) ending. These plays often have people falling in love, wearing disguises and generally getting all mixed up. *A Midsummer Night's Dream* is a comedy with fairies, humans and all sorts of funny goings-on.

TRAGEDIES with a sad ending and some grim bits along the way. *Romeo and Juliet* is a tragedy, because the young lovers, Romeo and Juliet (**SPOILER ALERT**) both die.

HISTORY plays about real people. These are based on true events and world leaders, such as Julius Caesar, the Roman general – or the English kings Henry V and Richard III. The Scottish king made famous by Shakespeare was called… sorry, not allowed to say. Macbeth – oops, that's done it!

Old Superstition

Did you know, actors often fear to mention the name 'Macbeth' as they believe the word brings bad luck? Instead they call it 'The Scottish Play'. Be warned, you are about to find out some of the foulest bits of 'the word that must not be spoken'.

Because many people in Shakespeare's time (including King James I) believed in the power of witches, *Macbeth* was a story that upset audiences. The play starts with three scary witches casting spells and telling Macbeth he will eventually become King of Scotland, as they stir their cauldron and add some foul ingredients...

WITCHES' BREW

Fillet of a fenny snake,
In the cauldron boil and bake;
Eye of newt and toe of frog,
Wool of bat and tongue of dog,
Adder's fork and blind-worm's sting,
Lizard's leg and howlet's wing,
For a charm of powerful trouble,
Like a hell-broth boil and bubble.
Cool it with a baboon's blood,
Then the charm is firm and good.
Scale of dragon, mashed fish eyes...
And that's my recipe for pies.
Our Witch MacPasty's great to scoff,
Welcome to this week's Bake-Off!

Unmentionable

The story goes that *Macbeth* was cursed from its opening night in 1606. The actor who was playing Lady Macbeth became mysteriously ill and Shakespeare himself had to step into his shoes. King James I, who asked Shakespeare to write *Macbeth*, attended the opening night. It was a flop and it wasn't performed for another 50 years.

Since 1606, there have been a string of deaths and 'bad things' connected to *Macbeth*. In 1667, the dark and gruesome tragedy was rewritten as a comic musical, with dancing and a flying ballet. This version, with three singing witches, was revived in 1703 when a terrible storm struck Britain. Bristol and London were wrecked, with many people killed. Was *Macbeth* to blame? Many believed so.

I call it the Scottish Play to avoid saying Macbeth... DOH!

Over the years, many actors playing Macbeth have fallen off the stage or been stabbed in the sword-fighting scenes. In one performance, the actor playing Macduff had his thumbs chopped off on stage. In 1849, there was a riot in which more than 30 people died at the Astor Place Opera House in New York, where 'The Scottish Play' was on.

In 1937, the famous actor Laurence Olivier lost his voice and almost died when a weight from the stage lights fell right beside him. The founder of the theatre, Lilian Baylis, had a heart attack and died the night before the play opened. Later a member of the audience was hit by a fragment of Olivier's sword and died of a heart attack.

During a World War 2 production with John Gielgud as Macbeth, one witch fell ill and died of a heart attack during the final rehearsal and the actor playing King Duncan also died. Another witch was dancing round the cauldron and suddenly collapsed and died on stage.
In 1947, a young actor playing Macbeth crawled off stage gasping, 'I've been stabbed'. He was taken to a hospital and died a month later.

The actor Charlton Heston had to ride a horse bareback in the first scene but suddenly rushed off stage, pointing at his backside and yelling: 'Get them off me!' The sweat of the horse, the heat and the chemicals on his clothes had caused serious burns to Heston's behind. Later, Macbeth's castle came down burning as planned, but the wind blew flames and smoke into the audience, causing a stampede. Oops. No wonder 'that play' has such a reputation!

Can it get any worse?

At the end of the play, Macbeth succeeds in becoming king but his life goes from bad to worse. Shakespeare wrote a speech to show how useless the king feels. It is one of the most famous speeches in literature, getting to the heart of how it must be to lose everything so that day after day seems totally meaningless…

To-morrow, and to-morrow,
and to-morrow,
Creeps in this petty pace from
day to day,
To the last syllable of
recorded time;
And all our yesterdays have
lighted fools
The way to dusty death. Out,
out, brief candle!
Life's but a walking shadow;
a poor player,
That struts and frets his hour
upon the stage,

And then is heard no more:
it is a tale
Told by an idiot,
full of sound and fury,
Signifying nothing.

(Macbeth, 5:5)

Time To Cheer Up

Knock, Knock.
Who's there?
Tom.
Tom who?
Tom R. O. and Tom R. O. and Tom R. O. creeps in this petty pace from day to day.

More Loopy Limericks

There once was a writer
named Will,
Who wrote with a pen
called a quill,
Some play scripts, at first he
Made very bloodthirsty...
Enough to make audiences ill*

(*GROSS ALERT: In 2014, a production of *Titus Andronicus* at the Globe Theatre in London reported more than 100 people fainting or leaving the theatre after being overcome by the on-stage gore.)

There once was a man
called Macbeth
Whose story will
shorten your breath.
Shakespeare told the lot
In a sickening plot
Packed full of foul
murder and death.

Did you hear of the
bad-tempered actor
Who, despite having tons of
X Factor,
Avoided her death scene
When playing Macbeth's Queen
So they brought down the
curtain and sacked her?

Did You Know?

The 'Knock knock, who's there?' joke began in *Macbeth*. The line is spoken by the porter who takes ages to open a door despite constant knocking. So, how about 3 cheesy knock-knocks for William?

Knock, knock!
Who's there?
William
William who?
Williamind my bike while I go to the shops?

Knock, knock!
Who's there?
William.
William who?
Williamind telling me what you thought of *Macbeth*?

Knock, knock!
Who's there?
Will.
Will who?
Will you stop all these cheesy knock, knock jokes as they're nothing like Shakespeare's 'Knock, knock! Who's there?' in *Macbeth*, anyway!

Shakespeare Shenanigans with Wow Words

EEK – time for a grammar lesson...

Have you heard anyone say, 'I was waiting with bated breath'? It means they were so eager, anxious, excited or frightened that they almost forgot to breathe.

'Bated breath' was just one of hundreds of expressions invented by Shakespeare.

'Bated' comes from the word 'abate', which means 'to get smaller'. So when you're waiting with bated (abated) breath, you're losing your breath and getting a bit tense.

It's nothing to do with 'baited' like when you bait a hook to catch a fish, eagerly waiting for a bite. Not many people know that.

Extra Cheesy Joke

Why did the cat swallow a lump of smelly cheese?

So it could wait by the mouse hole with baited breath. Get it?

Experts tell us the average speaker of English knows between 10,000-20,000 words. Shakespeare used over 31,500 different words in his writing. He probably knew another 35,000 so he was something of a wordius. (That's a word made-up here to describe a word genius. Impressed?)

Shakespeare actually invented over 1,700 of our common words by changing nouns into verbs, verbs into adjectives or connecting words never used together before.

'Scuffle', 'swagger', 'grovel' and 'undress' are words that Shakespeare gave us (though not all at once – what a scene that would be). 'Gloomy' and 'zany' are his, too. Clever, eh?

Mind Your Language

Because people spoke and wrote English in 1600 very differently from how we speak and write today, Shakespeare's speeches can often be difficult for us to understand. It's easy for us to miss his witty puns and sometimes disgusting jokes. English accents and the way we pronounce words have changed so much since Shakespeare wrote his plays that his jokes and rhymes don't always make sense to today's audiences.

Spellings didn't matter so much 400 years ago, probably because few people could read. In fact, Shakespeare didn't seem to bother about the spelling of his own name.

In the handful of signatures that have survived, the Bard never spelled his own name as 'William Shakespeare', using variations or abbreviations such as 'Willm Shakp', 'Willm Shakspere' and 'William Shakspeare'. So next time you spell a word incorrectly, you're in good company. Even geniuses don't always spell correctly!

JUST FOR THE RECORD –

If you shuffle up the letters in 'William Shakespeare' you can make 'I am a weakish speller'. And if you want to make more anagrams out of the Bard's name, here goes:

I'll make a wise phrase

Lame Swahili speaker

Hear me as I will speak

Can you think of any more?

Did You Know?

Olivia is the name of a character in *Twelfth Night*. Shakespeare was the first person to use the name with this spelling. It's the most popular name from a Shakespeare play still used today.

In *Twelfth Night* Olivia asks Viola 'Are you a comedian?' Written in 1616, this is one of the first records of 'comedian' used to mean 'comic actor'.

The word 'love' appears almost 2,200 times in the complete works of Shakespeare.

Many everyday phrases were first used by Shakespeare, such as 'vanish into thin air', 'in a pickle', 'be cruel to be kind', 'it's all Greek to me' and 'a tower of strength'.

Shakespeare made up all kinds of similes. That's just a way of comparing one thing to another, like 'as cold as a dead man's nose'. The one we still use from Shakespeare's play *Henry VI Part II* is 'as dead as a doornail'. You can't get much deader than a doornail after it's been bashed on the head and bent over at the end. After all, it can never be used again.

Messy Metaphor

A more unusual saying still used sometimes today comes from Hamlet. It is 'Hoist with his own petard'. Have you ever been hoist by your own petard?

This means to be caught out by your own plot – when a cunning plan backfires. A petard was a firework or a small bomb packed with gunpowder, so the expression really means you're blown up by your own bomb. Mind you, the French have a word related to petard: 'péter' – which means to fart. Imagine being hoist by one of those!

Talking of loud noises, bombs and **DEATH**, Shakespeare's plays are full of it. Brace yourself for some deadly facts. Look away now if you're squeamish…

There are about **100** deaths in all of Shakespeare's plays. **52** of those are by stabbing but there are plenty of other ways he kills off his characters.

In *Antony and Cleopatra*, Enobarbus dies of shame; in *A Winter's Tale* Antigonus is mauled by a bear; and in *Titus Andronicus* Chiron and Demetrius are baked into a pie, while Alarbus is dismembered, disembowelled and then burned on a fire. Anyone for a barbecue?

Cross Alert

More gruesome stuff...keep an eye out for the nasty bit...

In Shakespeare's *King Lear*, there's a gory torture scene when Regan (one of King Lear's three daughters) gouges out the eyes from the Earl of Gloucester. She seemed such a nice girl, too.

After one particularly grisly performance of the play, a newspaper reported: 'the graphic way Regan appears to use her mouth to suck out an "eye" and then spit it or allow it to fall on the stage has upset some theatregoers who have felt faint and needed fresh air before they can continue watching.' Yuck. Anyone for a pickled onion?

YUCK!

MORE SHAKESPEARE SAYINGS WE STILL OFTEN USE.

How many do you know and how many can you slip into your next conversation?

1 'Break the ice'

(*The Taming of the Shrew*)

2 'Brevity is the soul of wit'

(*Hamlet*)

3 'Refuse to budge an inch'

(*Measure for Measure*/*The Taming of the Shrew*)

4 'Eaten me out of house and home'

(*Henry IV Part II*)

5 'Forever and a day'

(*As You Like It*)

6 'For goodness' sake'

(*Henry VIII*)

7 'Foregone conclusion'

(*Othello*)

8 'Jealousy is the green-eyed monster'

(*Othello*)

9 'Heart of gold'

(*Henry V*)

10 'In my mind's eye'

(*Hamlet*)

11 'Kill with kindness'

(*The Taming of the Shrew*)

12 'Laughing stock'

(*The Merry Wives of Windsor*)

13 'Love is blind'

(*The Merchant of Venice*)

14 'Milk of human kindness'

(*Macbeth*)

15 'Set my teeth on edge'

(*Henry IV Part I*)

16 'Wear my heart upon my sleeve'

(*Othello*)

17 'Wild-goose chase'

(*Romeo and Juliet*)

Top Three Plays

According to different surveys, the most performed and most popular Shakespeare plays are:

A Midsummer Night's Dream

Hamlet

Romeo and Juliet

But do you know your Bottom from your Elbow?

(One is a weaver in *A Midsummer Night's Dream*, the other is a constable in *Measure for Measure*).

Here's a **TEST**. Which of the following is a genuine quote from one of these three plays?

1 'For never was a story of more magic
Than this midsummer madness –
though nothing tragic.'

2 'For never was a story of more woe
Than this of Juliet and her Romeo.'

3 'For never was a story of more sadness
Than this of Hamlet and a ghostly dadness.'

Read on to find the answer

A MIDSUMMER NIGHT'S DREAM

This play, with its fairies, magic and an enchanted wood (just outside Athens) is a favourite for performing outdoors in summer. Apparently, a performance in 1631 was on a Sunday, which was against the law. As a result, the actor playing Bottom had to be placed in the stocks for 12 hours, still wearing his ass's head.

Heard outside a theatre where Shakespeare's *A Midsummer Night's Dream* was being performed in 2013. 'I've paid a lot of money to see David Walliams's Bottom. It's meant to be very polished and funny.'

Note: Nick Bottom is a comic character in the play.

A ridiculous play

Samuel Pepys wrote a diary in the mid-1600s and he hated this play when he saw it in 1662: 'Then to the King's Theatre, where we saw *Midsummer Night's Dream*, which I had never seen before, nor shall ever again, for it is the most insipid, ridiculous play that ever I saw in my life. I saw, I confess, some good dancing and some handsome women, which was all my pleasure.'

FAMOUS LINE FROM THE PLAY:

'The course of true love never did run smooth.'

In other words, having a boyfriend or girlfriend can often cause problems! Lysander tells his girlfriend Hermia that they're not the only true lovers who've had big worries. Very true.

HAMLET

This marathon of a play can leave you exhausted and with a numb behind. After a 4½ hour drama with fights, ghosts and much else, four dead bodies are slumped on the stage at the end.

Hamlet is the longest of all Shakespeare's plays, with 29,551 words. Any actor playing the main character of Hamlet must learn 11,610 words. Phew.

HAMLET SPEAKS SOME OF SHAKESPEARE'S MOST WELL-KNOWN LINES, SO TAKE A DEEP BREATH AND HAVE A GO...

To be, or not to be,
that is the question:
Whether 'tis nobler in
the mind to suffer
The slings and arrows of
outrageous fortune
Or to take arms against
a sea of troubles,
And by opposing end them?

Later, Hamlet goes a bit crazy and does something terrible. Look away now if you faint at the sight of blood (and rats).

Hamlet kills Polonius, mistaking him for the King hiding behind a screen. Queen Gertrude, terrified that Hamlet is about to murder her, cries out for help. Polonius also cries for help, and Hamlet thinks the King has followed him, so thrusts his sword into the screen and kills Polonius on the other side. Oops.

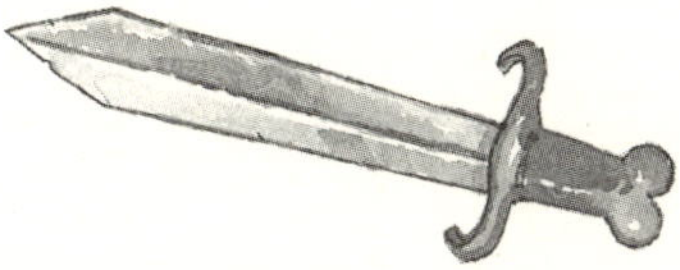

Hamlet: (Drawing sword) How now! A rat? Dead for a ducat, dead!

(Stabs through the screen)

Polonius: (Behind the screen) O, I am slain! (Falls and dies)

Queen Gertrude: O me, what hast thou done?

Have you ever had one of those kinds of days?

Eventually Hamlet finds the skull of Yorick, the royal jester, in a graveyard. Holding the skull, he speaks the line: 'Alas, poor Yorick! I knew him, Horatio: a fellow of infinite jest, of most excellent fancy.'

Yorick doesn't look impressed!

Did you know *Hamlet* inspired *The Lion King*? Just change Denmark for Africa and swap people for lions and hey presto… an evil uncle strikes again.

A proud king (Mufasa) is killed 'accidentally' by his evil, power-hungry brother (Scar), and after a time away from the kingdom, the prince and rightful heir (Simba) returns to bring the truth to light. The film even includes the ghostly vision of Mufasa, and Simba's pair of fast-talking friends Timon and Pumbaa (Rosencrantz and Guildenstern in the Shakespeare play). Mind you, *The Lion King* has a happier ending and a few jolly songs along the way. Hakuna matata!

ROMEO AND JULIET

Romeo and Juliet is based on an Italian folktale, which Shakespeare adapted. This love story (**ANOTHER SPOILER ALERT** – it doesn't end well) is so popular that there have been more than 27 operas written based on the play. There have also been ballets, jazz music, musicals, movies, modern music, a Twitter series and paintings as well as other art works all based on this tragic tale:

'For never was a
story of more woe
Than this of Juliet
and her Romeo.'

The problem is all down to two families being bitter enemies but two of their teens falling in love. Juliet wishes that Romeo was from another family with another name: 'That which we call a rose by any other name would smell as sweet.' In that line Shakespeare was also having a dig at the rival Rose Theatre up the road, which apparently stank to high heaven.

One of the most famous scenes in the play is the balcony scene, where Romeo and Juliet declare their love for each other – her from her balcony and him from the ground below.

'Oh Romeo, where have you been?'
Cried Juliet, a love-smitten teen,
'Climb up to these heights,
But don't rip your tights
Or you'll ruin our balcony scene!'*

** This isn't the real dialogue!*

Pun Time

Apparently, two people each claim to live in the building where Shakespeare wrote *Romeo & Juliet*. They should put a plaque on both their houses.

(In case you didn't know… It should be 'a plague on both your houses', as in Mercutio's death speech: 'I am hurt. A plague o' both your houses.')

Did You Know?

The original title that William Shakespeare chose for *Romeo and Juliet* was actually *The Most Excellent and Lamentable Tragedy of Romeo and Juliet*. Not quite so catchy.

Jester Jokery (MANGLING THE BARD)

Warning – these jokes are cheesier than a truck full of Cheesy Wotsits.

RICHARD III

In Shakespeare's play *Richard lll*, the king cries out, 'A horse! A horse! My kingdom for a horse!' after his horse is killed in battle, leaving him at the mercy of his enemies. Many years later, when King Richard's bones were discovered buried under a carpark in Leicester in 2015, the headlines read 'A Porsche! A Porsche! My kingdom for a Porsche!'

Another well-known line from this play is 'Now is the winter of our discontent, made glorious summer by this sun of York', written by Shakespeare in 1594. The words have since been mangled into this terrible joke:

Richard III decided to take a break from battles and ran a camping shop in Wales. During a season of terrible weather, sales in the store dropped badly. To get more customers, he decided to hold a massive sale with a barbecue and hog roast. The banner proclaimed: 'Now is the winter of our discount tents, made glorious summer by this leg of pork.' Doh!

THE MERCHANT OF VENICE

Shakespeare gave the character Portia these lines in *The Merchant of Venice* – to show how kindness and forgiveness should be given freely:

'The quality of mercy is
not strained.
It droppeth as the gentle
rain from heaven
Upon the place beneath.'

Then came the cheesy joke...

An Australian on walkabout got very lost and eventually came upon a little town in the outback called Mersey. He staggered into a grubby café and asked for a cold drink.

'Sorry, mate,' the waiter said, 'the refrigerator doesn't work. All our cans are warm. I'll bring you some of our special blend of tea. It's very refreshing.'

When a mug of tea arrived, the explorer looked at it with disgust. There were big brown clumps in it. 'Yeech. What's this?'

The waiter replied, 'It's our special tea made from local Koala bears.'

'But why the big brown clumps?' the man asked, 'have you never heard of a tea-strainer?'

'Ah,' said the waiter, in a rich Shakespearean voice, 'the Koala-tea of Mersey is not strained.'

A rose by any other name would smell as sweet

There was once a great Shakespearean actor who could no longer remember his lines. At last, a theatre was prepared to give him a chance in an unknown play.

The director said, 'This is the most important part, and you have only one line. You walk on the stage at the opening, carrying a rose. You hold the rose to your nose with just one finger and thumb, sniff the rose deeply and then say the line "Ah, I have picked my own beauty to delight my nose."'

The actor was thrilled. All day before the play he practised his line over and over again. Finally, the time came for the curtain to rise. The actor walked onto the stage and, with great passion, delivered the line, 'Ah, I have picked my own nose to delight my beauty.'

The theatre erupted, the audience screaming with laughter as the director shouted from the wings, 'You blithering nincompoop!'

The actor was bewildered, 'What happened, did I forget my line?'

'Not only did you get it the wrong way round,' screamed the director, 'but you forgot the rose!'

The following year they gave the actor one last chance. The director wanted him to walk on grandly and say dramatically, 'Hark! I hear the cannon roar!'

After much worry, the actor decided to take the role. The opening night arrived, and while he waited in the wings, the actor muttered to himself 'Hark! I hear the cannon roar! Hark! I hear the cannon roar!'

The time for the entrance finally came and, as the actor made his appearance, there was a loud BOOOOM! He turned and stuttered, 'What the heck was that?'

Anne: Prithee, fair William – thine dinner be on the table. Oysters and mash.

William: Why then, the world's mine oyster.

Anne: Ye what, mine poppet?

William: If molluscs be the food of love, I'll have fish and chips.

Anne: Mushy peas with that?

William: Hmmm… methinks…. methinks… methinks…

Anne: What dost thou thinketh, sweet William?

William: To pea or not to pea, that is the question.

Anne: The chamber pot be under yon second-best bed.*

* Did you know that in Shakespeare's will, he left to his wife 'my second-best bed with furniture'? The 'furniture' was the bedclothes. This is all he left his wife, and the only time she was mentioned in his will. Maybe the mattress was stuffed with cash. Maybe not. Thanks a lot, William.

Fooling Around

Shakespeare loved to play with words and tease an audience with puns, patter and points to ponder. In many plays long ago, a clown figure known as a fool or jester would appear in some scenes to bring a change of mood and a few laughs.

Shakespearean fools were often clever peasants who used their wits to outdo the grander characters. That made them popular with the groundlings in the audience, but also among some royal visitors. Queen Elizabeth I was a particular admirer of the popular actor who played fools in Shakespeare's comedies such as:

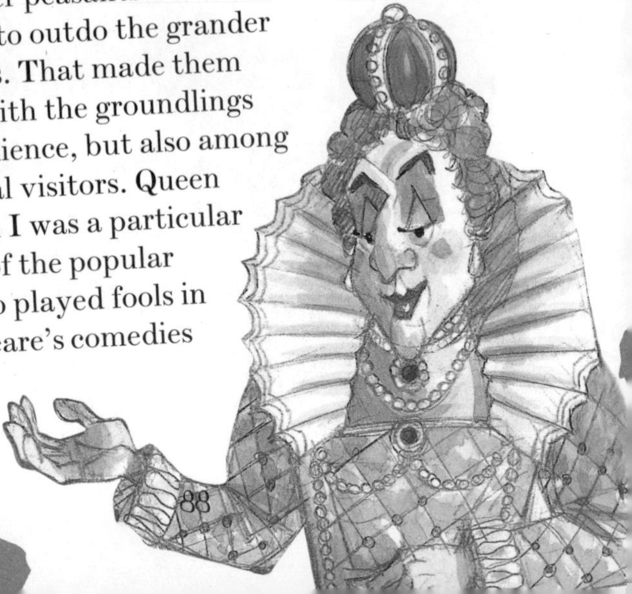

Lavanche in *All's Well That Ends Well*

Touchstone in *As You Like it*

The Dromio twins in *The Comedy of Errors*

Costard in *Love's Labour's Lost*

Pompey in *Measure for Measure*

Puck in *A Midsummer Night's Dream*

Grumio in *The Taming of The Shrew*

Feste in *Twelfth Night*

Don't Be Fooled

The title 'fool' or 'clown' can be a bit misleading because we tend to think such characters must be simple or stupid. But they were more like stand-up comedians with sharp and witty comments to make who could run rings round their 'betters'.

A fool's job was to entertain but also to speak or sing a few pearls of wisdom – to make an audience think as well as giggle. So if anyone ever calls you a fool, that must mean you're really clever!

Limerick

It isn't very funny playing the fool,
I perform in Shakespeare's dramas,
as a rule,
To display wisdom and wit,
Then show off, just a bit...
But it isn't very funny being a fool.

It's a very serious business as a clown,
And always being witty gets me down.
All the time I have to jest,
Ridiculously dressed.
No, it isn't very funny being a clown.

While audiences chuckle,
My confidence can buckle
But still I must perform
and not break down.
It really is abysmal,
People laugh when I feel dismal...
No, it isn't very funny being a clown.

It isn't very funny playing the fool,
I'm the butt of all the jokes
and that's so cruel.
I'm meant to raise a laugh,
Speaking words too wise by half...
No, it isn't very funny being a fool.

It isn't very funny being a clown,
Being recognised and cheered
around the town,
When people shout abuse
or hurl tomato juice,
No, it isn't very funny being a clown.

It isn't very funny being a clown,
Acting in green tights or
sparkly gown,
It really isn't easy
When I look and sound so cheesy,
No, it isn't very funny being a clown.

In Shakespeare's plays I tremble,
When such rowdy crowds assemble
And all I want to do is just lie
down.
But I have to learn the script,
No stanza can be skipped,
No, it isn't very funny being a clown.

The other actors pester me,
Why can't they let a jester be
Allowed to wear nice clothes
or golden crown?
It really isn't pleasant,
As they treat me like a peasant,
No, it isn't very funny being a clown.

YAY! Each time I take my bow,
The crowds adore me now!
They clap me more than
anyone around.
In fact, it's rather funny,
Some people throw me money...
Well, it can be rather funny as a clown!

There's nothing foolish about a fool!

Random Riveting(ish) Records

BEST-SELLING playwright

Shakespeare remains the world's best-selling playwright, with sales of his plays and poetry believed to have reached over four billion copies in the 400 years since his death.

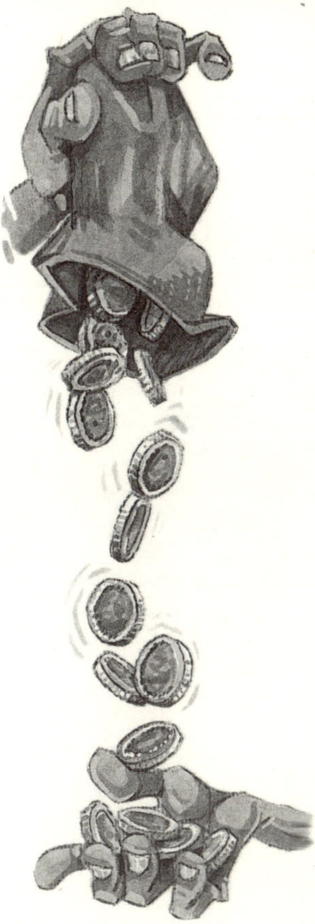

Most expensive literature by Shakespeare

One of only five copies of Shakespeare's First Folio, dated 1623, was sold at Christie's, New York City, USA, in 2001 for $6,166,000 (£4,156,947). It remains the highest price ever paid for a 17th-century book. Just imagine how rich Shakespeare would be if he were still alive today.

Biggest Cast

The most people performing Shakespeare on a single day were 7,104 schoolchildren, as part of the Shakespeare Schools Festival around the UK in 2005. 92 theatres hosted 368 productions. Wow!

LONGEST performance

Adrian Hilton recited the complete works of Shakespeare in 110 hours and 46 minutes during a 'Bardathon' at the Shakespeare Festival on the site of Shakespeare's Globe Theatre in London, from 16th to 21st July, 1987.

MOST FILMED author

Shakespeare's plays and sonnets have been adapted into 420 feature films and TV-movie versions. *Hamlet* has appealed most to film makers with 79 versions, followed by *Romeo and Juliet* with 52 and *Macbeth*, filmed 36 times. Hollywood and Bollywood have adapted Shakespeare into all kinds of spectacular musicals, too.

DEATH by Shakespeare

Although Shakespeare is popular all over the world, there was a time when the people of New York must have blamed him for mess, mayhem and murder. Some called Shakespeare the Bird Bard because he mentioned many different types of bird in his plays. Unfortunately, someone decided to take them all to New York.

In 1890 Eugene Scheiffelin imported 60 starlings from England (and a further 40 the following year). As a Shakespeare fan, Scheiffelin wanted America to be the home of each bird species featured in the works of the bard. Big mistake.

The starlings thrived rather too well in Central Park and soon out-numbered the local birdlife, becoming a major pest. In 1960, an aeroplane setting off from Boston Airport stirred up a flock of 10,000 starlings on the runway. It flew straight into them, which choked the engines and brought the aeroplane down. The crash killed 62 people.

Foul Fate

In 1864, the Shakespearean actor John Wilkes Booth starred as Mark Antony in a performance of Shakespeare's *Julius Caesar* at New York City's Winter Garden Theatre. It raised money to place a statue of Shakespeare on Central Park's Literary Walk.

Five months later, on April 14, 1865, John Wilkes Booth made a more devastating performance at Ford's Theatre in Washington. Just like the part his brother played as Brutus, he assassinated the leader of a nation. He shot and killed the president, Abraham Lincoln – who also happened to be a great fan of William Shakespeare. Booth was tracked down and shot twelve days later. A real news story seemed just like a Shakespearean tragedy.

Today the Royal Shakespeare Company sells more than half a million tickets a year for Shakespeare productions at their theatres in Stratford-upon-Avon, London and Newcastle. That's big business – with millions more tourists visiting landmarks and all the other theatres putting on Shakespeare's plays. The Bard is a megabucks industry more than ever before.

The RSC has a few quirky secrets up its frilly sleeve:

1. The company has its own armoury and makes its own wigs. Belly hair from yaks is used to make the beards.

2. The technical crew can fly in props from above the stage with 99% accuracy. They tested this once with an egg – splat!

3. In the reading room, there is a Shakespearean insult chair which shouts abuse at you when you sit on it, and copies of reviews of all of the RSC's shows.

All the world's a stage

Did you hear about the set designer who was sacked from the Royal Shakespeare Company for not producing anything at all?

He left quietly, without making a scene.

Grand Finale (EPILOGUE)

SONG AND DANCE

The Hokey-Cokey (Shakespeare-style)

O fleeting is the foot that thou
dost tread within,
Betwixt its backward gesture,
thence returneth whence begin.
Forsooth, again thy left foot it
doth quaver o'er the line
And thou dost shudder nobly -
yonder shimmy, oft divine.
Whereupon thou then in rapture
Hokey-Cokey dance,
How wondrous well gyrateth
thou with hips-a-spin, perchance.
In truth, carouse thy shapely leg,
cross-gartered ne'r worn out,
Thus verily, I say, prithee,
'tis what it's all about.' Oi!

A FINAL SONG
(try the tune of Greensleeves)

The words of Shakespeare soothe the soul,
Especially calm and quiet...
But if music be the food of love,
You'd best go on a diet.

The words of Shakespeare touch the heart,
At breakfast, try a sonnet...
But best avoid *Hamlet* and eggs,
In case you get yolk on it.

The words of Shakespeare stir the blood,
You may well shed a tear
Or take up arms and grab a lance...
Then you Will Shake-a-spear!

William Shakespeare Timeline

1564 William Shakespeare is born in Stratford-upon-Avon, England to Mary and John Shakespeare. He is their third child out of eight.

1571 William starts grammar school in Stratford at the age of 7.

1582 He marries Anne Hathaway, a farmer's daughter who is 26 years old (8 years older than him).

1583 Their first child, Susanna, is born. She lives to the age of 66.

1585 Their twins are born. The boy, Hamnet, dies at the age of 11. The girl, Judith, lives to be 77 years old – a very good age for those times.

1585 Shakespeare leaves Stratford for London to start his career in the theatre at the age of 21.

1593 He starts writing sonnets as a plague spreads through London.

1594 He sets up the Lord Chamberlain's Men, an acting company.

1594 He writes *Romeo & Juliet* and *A Midsummer Night's Dream*

1596 Hamnet dies. William buys a large house in Stratford called New Place. His company of actors move to the Swan Theatre on Bankside when London's authorities ban the public presentation of plays within the city limits of London.

1599 The Globe Theatre opens in Southwark, south of the River Thames. Shakespeare is a part owner.

1603 Queen Elizabeth I dies. James I becomes king. Both enjoyed Shakespeare's plays. James renames the company The King's Men.

1613 The Globe Theatre burns to the ground. It is rebuilt and able to open in the following year – but demolished 30 years later by the Puritans (who disapproved of theatre).

1616 (23rd April, St George's Day) Shakespeare dies after a few days of fever at the age of 52. He is buried in Stratford-upon-Avon.

Why all the fuss?

A world without William Shakespeare would be a very different place. He didn't just change the English language, he made it possible for ordinary people to learn about history, many different places and 'being human'.

His amazing skill at showing the range of human emotions in simple yet profound verse is why he still speaks to us today. If you cannot find words to express how you feel about love, loss, jealousy, joy or growing old, Shakespeare can speak for you. He was also the master of truly foul and cheesy facts and jokes!

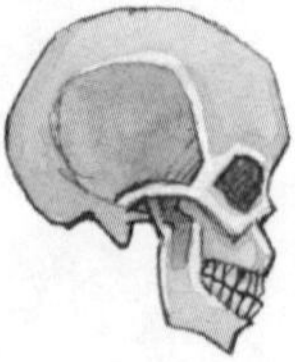

A final quick guide to 6 popular Shakespeare plays:

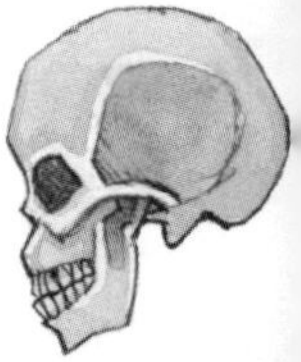

1. **Hamlet**
   everyone dies
2. **Macbeth**
   everyone dies
3. **King Lear**
   everyone dies
4. **Romeo and Juliet**
   everyone dies
5. **All's Well That Ends Well**
   everyone lives
6. **As You Like It**
   confusing chases around a forest (the boy actor had to play Rosalind, a woman who pretends to be a man pretending to be a woman!)

FAREWELL FROM THE BARD

All the world's a stage,
And all the men and women merely players.
They have their exits and their entrances
And one man in his time plays many parts.

As You Like It

Our revels now are ended.
These our actors,
As I foretold you, were all
spirits and
Are melted into air, into thin air:
And, like the baseless fabric of
this vision,
The cloud-capp'd towers, the
gorgeous palaces,
The solemn temples, the great
globe itself,
Yea, all which it inherit,
shall dissolve

And, like this insubstantial
pageant faded,
Leave not a rack behind.
We are such stuff
As dreams are made on,
and our little life
Is rounded with a sleep.

The Tempest

Good night, good night!
Parting is such sweet sorrow
That I shall say good night
till it be morrow.

Romeo & Juliet

The Bard Returns

In 2016, coffee shop customers were stunned to see the ghostly figure of William Shakespeare on the 400th anniversary of his death in Prescot, Merseyside. Shocked pedestrians reported seeing the 'freaky face' of the bard peering down on them through a window of the café as they walked past on the street below.

But the freaky phantom figure turned out to be no more than a cardboard cut-out of Shakespeare, put up by the café owner to mark his special anniversary. Its spooky shadow caused quite a stir and more than a storm in a teacup when customers and shoppers were convinced it was a 'ghost they saw before them' – or as the man himself would have said:

'Horses did neigh, and
dying men did groan,
And ghosts did shriek and
squeal about the streets'

Julius Caesar

EEEK – Don't have nightmares!

Verily, if thou'st survived some of the truly foul facts and cheesy jokes in this book, take a look at the other wacky titles in this revolting series. They're all guaranteed to make thee groan and squirm like never before. Share them with thine friends **AT THINE OWN RISK!**

'Tis time to test thee and see if thou hast paid attention...

QUIZ

1. On what day did Shakespeare supposedly die?

a) His wedding anniversary

b) His birthday

c) Christmas Eve

2. What is Shakespeare's longest play?

a) Hamlet

b) Othello

c) The Neverending Story

3. How many words did Shakespeare invent?

a) Almost 3,000

b) Almost 5,000

c) None – he was rubbish with words

4. Why was The Globe theatre closed between 1592 and 1594?

a) Redecoration

b) Censorship

c) Plague

5. Who played the women's parts in plays in Shakespeare's time?

a) Women, obviously

b) Boys

c) Horses

6. Which play is believed to be cursed?

a) A Midsummer Night's Dream

b) Antony and Cleopatra

c) Macbeth

7. What type of animal's head does Nick Bottom wear in *A Midsummer Night's Dream*?

a) An ass

b) A giraffe

c) A pig

8. What did Shakespeare leave his wife in his will?

a) The cutlery

b) His second-best bed

c) His DVD collection

9. How many tickets does the Royal Shakespeare Company sell each year?

a) 500,000

b) 2 million

c) 45

10. In *Titus Andronicus*, what foodstuff are two murder victims made into?

a) Lasagne

b) Soup

c) A pie

Answers:

1= b
2= a
3= a
4= c
5= b
6= c
7= a
8= b
9= a
10= c

GLOSSARY

Anagram: a word or phrase made from another by changing the order of the letters

Assassination: murdering an important person by a surprise or secret attack

Bard: a writer skilled at composing and presenting dramatic verses

Ducat: a gold coin once used in various European countries

Insipid: lacking in taste and flavour

Metaphor: a figure of speech where a word or phrase meaning one thing is used in place of another to suggest a similarity between them

Stocks: a timber frame with holes to contain the feet or feet and hands of a wrongdoer as public punishment

Toupee: a small wig worn to cover a bald patch

INDEX

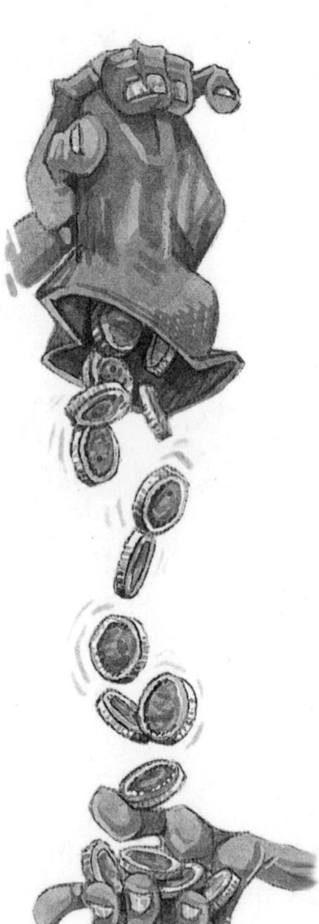

I finished reading this Truly Foul & Cheesy book on:

........../........../..........